Editing by Valerie Sweeten

ISBN-13: 978-1727066692

ISBN-10: 1727066693

# CLEOPATRA THE WISE

## By

## T.L. JOHNSON

TO MY MOTHER

THE WISEST PERSON I KNOW

LOVE ALWAYS

Of all his children, the pharaoh liked his daughter, Cleopatra, the best. She was kind and compassionate, but something else made her his favorite.

One day, Cleopatra's father gathered all his children together in the royal palace.

"My children, I am going away on important business for three weeks. I will need one of you to rule in my absence." His sons, who were excited, asked, "Father, who will rule the kingdom while you are away?"

The pharaoh said, "You boys are very strong and very brave, but Cleopatra will manage my kingdom. Serve her as you would me."

The pharaoh's sons were insulted. "Cleopatra is just a girl. How can she run the entire kingdom?"

"My sons, you have so much to learn. You will soon see why I chose her." The pharaoh replied.

Cleopatra was angry when her brothers convinced her to give them control of the kingdom, but felt she loved her brothers and wanted them to be happy.

"Cleo, you're just a girl,

and everyone knows girls are too emotional to make big decisions.

We'll show you how to run the kingdom the right way." Reluctantly she agreed.

"Why have you done this?" Cleopatra asked.

"This will impress Father," one brother said. "He will be pleased with how much surplus food we have in the palace."

Her other brother chimed in "You're just a girl. You wouldn't understand."

The second week, the brothers had another idea and increased the workload of their workers.

The third week, the brothers had their best idea yet and paid the workers less money.

"Why have you done this?" Cleopatra asked.

"Father will be pleased by how much gold we have saved the kingdom," the brothers said. "You're just a girl. You wouldn't understand."

But Cleopatra understood that the workers wouldn't have enough money to take care of their families.

Cleopatra was so angry that she stormed off and didn't stop walking until she reached her favorite garden. She sat on a bench and wept.

Suddenly, an old woman appeared out of nowhere.

"What's wrong, Princess Cleopatra?" The old woman asked.

"Our kingdom is falling apart! My brothers will not listen to me." "They have not listened because you have not spoken."

"What do you mean?"

"I mean your father put you in charge for a reason. You must find that reason." The old woman replied.

19

Cleopatra thought long and hard.

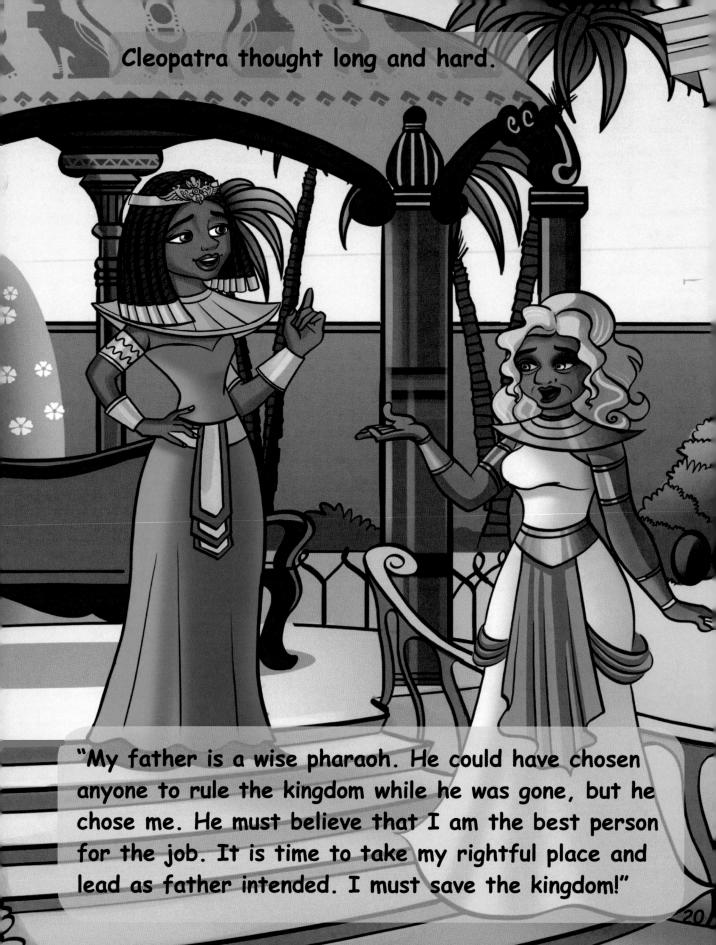

"My father is a wise pharaoh. He could have chosen anyone to rule the kingdom while he was gone, but he chose me. He must believe that I am the best person for the job. It is time to take my rightful place and lead as father intended. I must save the kingdom!"

Cleopatra rushed back to the palace to find an angry mob in front of the palace banging on the door of the castle. They shouted at Cleopatra's brothers trapped inside.

"We refuse to work!"

"You treat us unfairly!"

"We need food!"

In the throne room, her brothers argued amongst themselves.

"We should give them less money and less food!"

"We should lock them up!"

"No!" said Cleopatra. "That is not how Father would run the kingdom!"

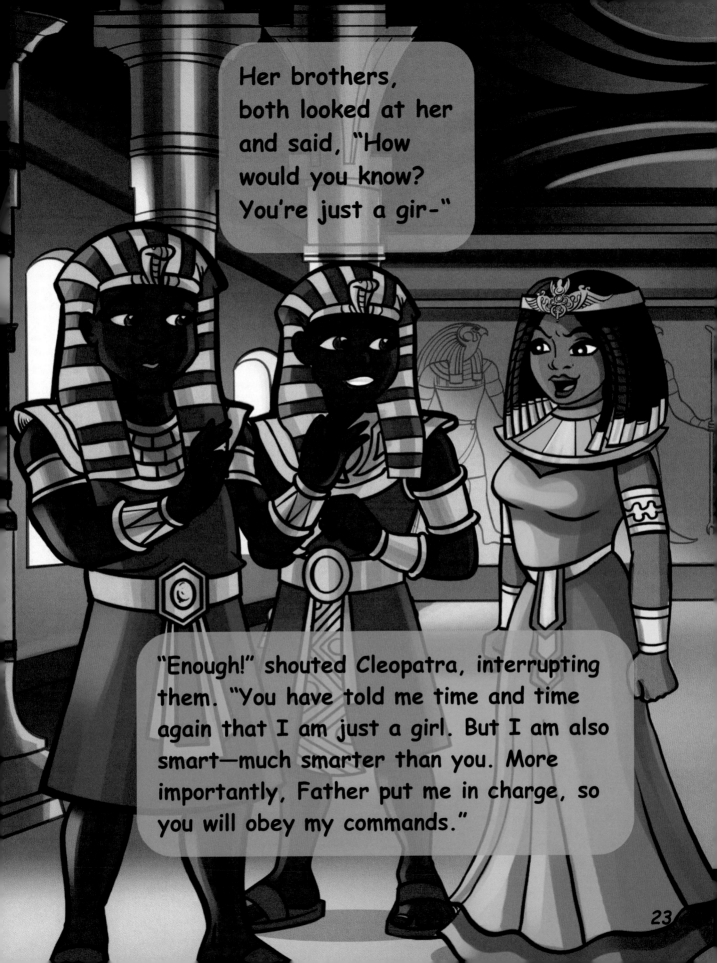

Her brothers, both looked at her and said, "How would you know? You're just a gir-"

"Enough!" shouted Cleopatra, interrupting them. "You have told me time and time again that I am just a girl. But I am also smart—much smarter than you. More importantly, Father put me in charge, so you will obey my commands."

By now, the mob had broken into the palace and were looking for her scared brothers.

Terrified, they both turned to her and asked, "What should we do, Cleopatra?"

Cleopatra smiled. She knew she had come up with a fair solution to solve all of the kingdom's problems. "First, return the food supply to normal so the workers will be strong. Second, reduce the hours they have to work so they can spend time with their families. And finally, pay them fairly for their work so they are happy."

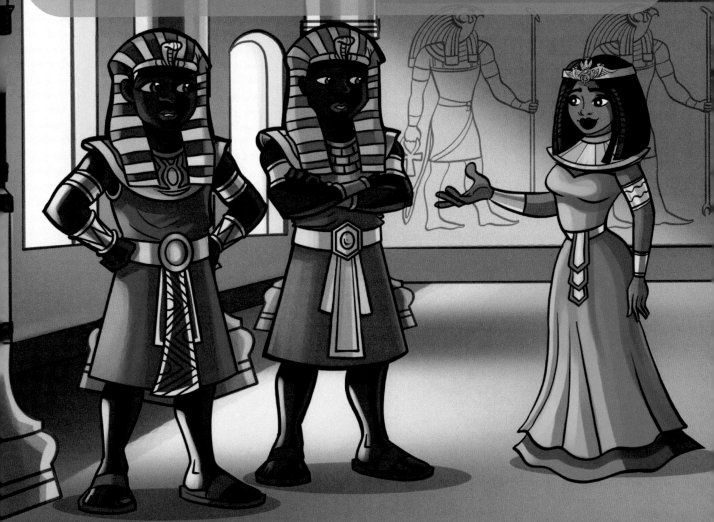

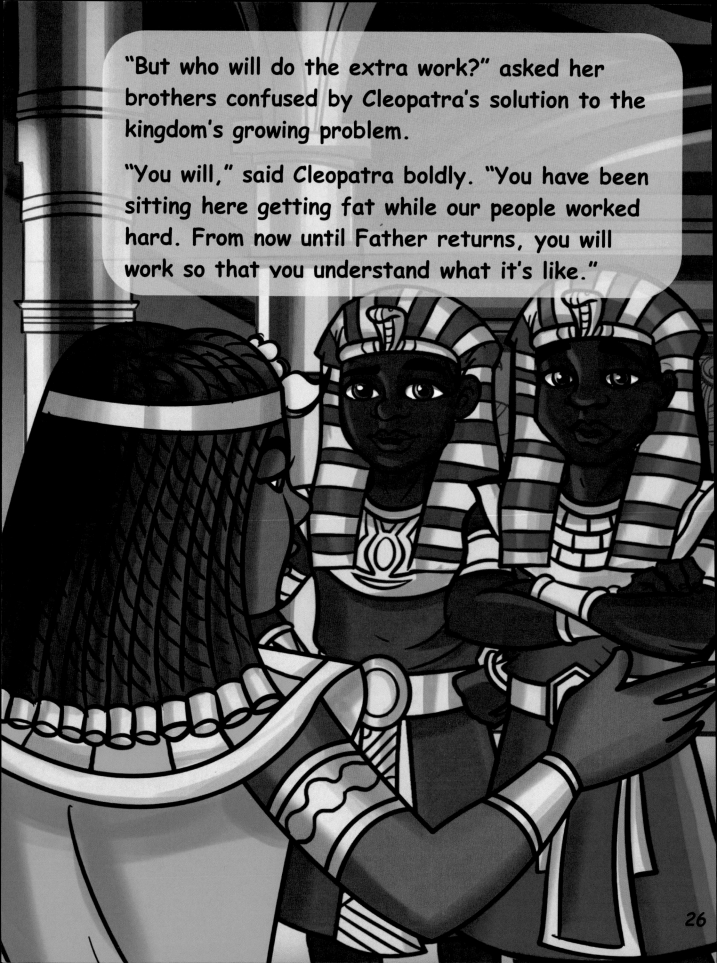

"But who will do the extra work?" asked her brothers confused by Cleopatra's solution to the kingdom's growing problem.

"You will," said Cleopatra boldly. "You have been sitting here getting fat while our people worked hard. From now until Father returns, you will work so that you understand what it's like."

Just then, the old woman reappeared and revealed herself to be one of the Ancient Queens. "I am Hathor and I am proud of you, Cleopatra. You have ruled the kingdom like a true leader."

"Thank you," said Cleopatra. "I just had to believe in myself."

When the pharaoh returned, he was delighted to find his kingdom in order. All of the work was done ahead of schedule, the people were happy, and her brothers were humbled.

"You have done a magnificent job my daughter!" The pharaoh said. "You even taught your brothers a thing or two."

"Thank you father," she replied. "I doubted myself at first, but then I figured it out and took charge and we worked it all out!"

Made in the USA
Middletown, DE
06 January 2022

57934901R00018